The Feather

by Dot Cleeve
illustrated by Kim Harley

Tamarind Ltd

For Jessica, Joshua, Benjamin and Esme
who enjoy finding feathers

and for Priory Primary, 1992-1998

Published by Tamarind Ltd, 2003
PO Box 52
Northwood
Middx HA6 1UN
UK

Text © Dot Cleeve
Illustrations © Kim Harley
Edited by Simona Sideri

ISBN 1 870516 61 3

Printed in Singapore

Near her home by the river
under a tree
Paula found a feather.

"Is this your feather?"
she asked a swan.

"No," hissed the swan.
"My feathers are snowy white.
Here's one of mine.

Look through it and you will see
the snow-capped mountains of the north and
pale, ice-cold skies."

The swan swept away.
Paula put the white feather in her bag.

Further down the bank
a moorhen looked after her babies.
"Whose feather is this?" Paula called out to her.

"I don't know,"
cackled the moorhen.

"Have one of my glossy black feathers.
Look through it and spy the night sky
holding the moon and
millions of stars above the world."

The moorhen paddled away.
Paula put the black feather in her bag.

A shy kingfisher peeked out of his hole in the bank.

"Is this your feather?" Paula asked.

"No… My best feathers are sapphire blue.

Look through one of mine and see
children playing on beaches,
palm trees waving to the skies and
divers in the deep."

Paula put the blue feather in her bag.

Along the rugged path by the grassy bank
a wagtail hopped into view.

"Can you tell me whose feather this is?"
"No," said the wagtail. "My feathers are a sunny yellow.

Look through this one to see
a lumpy, bumpy, sometimes grumpy
camel caravan."

The wagtail wagged its tail and sped off.
Paula put the yellow feather in her bag.

"Could this feather be yours?" said Paula,
as a pheasant hopped briskly by.
"No," squawked the pheasant.
"My feathers are copper brown
and beautiful.

Take one of mine if you like. See a farm
with a tractor ploughing furrows in the fields
for food for us to eat."

Paula stuffed the brown feather
into her bag and the pheasant
flew away.

Then a peacock came strutting along.
"Is this feather yours?" asked Paula.
"Of course not!" screeched the peacock.
"My feathers gleam with all the colours
of the rainbow.

Take a look through the eye
and see sunken treasure
in all its shimmering
beauty."

The peacock strutted
away.
Paula put the long,
colourful feather
in her bag.

Slowly, an enormous seagull flew down onto the bank.

"Is this your feather?" asked Paula.

"Yes," squawked the seagull.
"My feathers are grey like the mist at the dawn of time,
before there were colours in the world….
Keep it to remind you of that grey time, long, long ago."

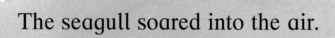

The seagull soared into the air.

Paula put the feathers
in a row. "I know just what
I shall do," she thought.

Moorhen

Kingfisher

Swan

Peacock

Wagtail

Pheasant

Seagull

"I shall thread them into my hat…
Then, when I wear it, I will see
all the colours that brighten up
our world!"

OTHER TAMARIND TITLES

The Bush – NEW for 2003
Boots for a Bridesmaid – new edition for 2003
Dizzy's Walk
Zia the Orchestra
Mum's Late
Rainbow House
Starlight
Marty Monster
Jessica
Yohance and the Dinosaurs
Kofi and the Butterflies

FOR OLDER READERS, AGED 9–12
Black Profile Series:
Benjamin Zephaniah
Lord Taylor of Warwick
Dr Samantha Tross
Malorie Blackman
Jim Brathwaite
Baroness Patricia Scotland of Asthal
Chinwe Roy

The Life of Stephen Lawrence

AND FOR YOUNGER CHILDREN
The Best Mum NEW for 2003
The Best Toy NEW for 2003
Are We There Yet? – new edition for 2003
Time for Bed – new edition for 2003
Let's Feed the Ducks
Let's Go to Bed
Let's Have Fun
Let's Go to Playgroup
Where's Gran?
Toyin Fay
Dave and the Tooth Fairy
Kim's Magic Tree
Time to Get Up
Finished Being Four
ABC – I Can Be
I Don't Eat Toothpaste Anymore
Giant Hiccups